panda series

**PANDA books are for young readers
making their own way
through books.**

O'BRIEN SERIES FOR YOUNG READERS

 panda cubs

 pandas

 panda legends

 flyers

Muckeen and the Big Freeze

• Words and pictures •

FERGUS LYONS

THE O'BRIEN PRESS
DUBLIN

First published 2011 by The O'Brien Press Ltd,
12 Terenure Road East, Dublin 6, Ireland.
Tel: +353 1 4923333; Fax: +353 1 4922777
E-mail: books@obrien.ie
Website: www.obrien.ie

ISBN: 978-1-84717-243-3

British Library Cataloguing-in-Publication Data
A catalogue reference for this title is available from the British Library.

The O'Brien Press receives assistance from

1 2 3 4 5 6 7 8 9 10
11 12 13 14 15 16 17

Typesetting, layout, editing, design: The O'Brien Press Ltd
Printed and bound by CPI Cox and Wyman Ltd.
The paper used in this book is produced using pulp from managed forests.

Can YOU spot the panda
hidden in the story?

Muckeen loved his bed.

It was only a
big heap of straw.
But Muckeen thought
it was **wonderful**.

Early one morning
in the middle of winter
something woke
Muckeen.

There was something
rustling in the straw.
He wondered what was
making the noise.

Muckeen sat straight up
in the bed.

What could it be?

Then he found out.

It was a family of field mice.

Muckeen knew them well.

He was delighted to see them.
He loved it when his friends
came to visit.

It was winter and
it was cold outside.
The mice had come
into the shed
to try to get warm.

Suddenly Muckeen noticed
snowflakes
on the mice.

'It must be snowing outside,'
thought Muckeen.
He had been looking forward
to snow for ages.

'Yippee!' he thought.
'The first snow of winter.'

Muckeen jumped out of bed
and ran to the window.
He stood on a bucket
and looked out.
Yes!
Snow was falling.
Really heavy snow.

As soon as it eased up a bit
Muckeen could go outside
to play.

He stayed at the window
watching the snow.
He was day-dreaming about
how much fun it was
going to be.

Muckeen dreamed of skiing
down the hill in the Big Field.

But he didn't know
how to ski,
and he didn't have
a pair of skis.

Outside, the snow fell
on and on and on.
Muckeen got tired of waiting.
Would it ever **stop**?
A cold wind from the north
began to blow the snow
into big drifts.

Muckeen waited for ages,
but it was no good.
The snow did not stop.

Muckeen got into bed
with the mice
to wait for the weather
to improve.

Soon they were all asleep.

It was late evening before
they woke up again.

It was growing dark.
Mrs Farmer still had not
brought Muckeen
his dinner of
sloppy stuff
in a bucket.

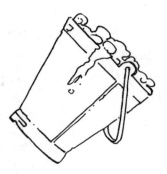

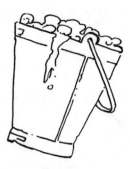

Muckeen was worried.
What if there was
no dinner at all?

That had **never** happened
to him before.

Muckeen tried to get
a drink of water
from the tap in his shed.
Nothing came out.
The pipes were
frozen solid.

It was so cold
there was frost and ice
on the inside of the window.

The day was almost over.
Still the snow kept falling.
Now it had turned into
a real blizzard.

Muckeen tried to push open
the door of his shed.

It would not budge.

The storm had piled snow up against the shed door. Muckeen was trapped.

Things were looking BAD.

Muckeen was SHIVERING.

He was HUNGRY.

He was COLD.

And he wanted

HIS DINNER.

It was almost dark
when Muckeen and the mice
heard a scraping sound
somewhere outside.

The mice heard it first.

Scrape! Scrape! Scrape!

It was coming nearer.

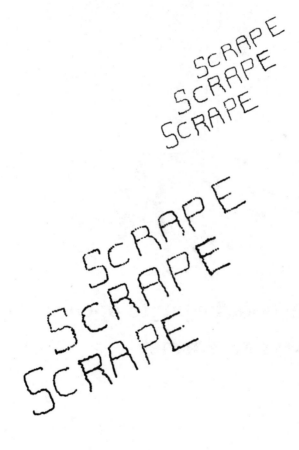

The door began to open slowly.

It was Mr Farmer.

He had a shovel in his hand.

He had cleared a path
through the snow
from the farmhouse
to Muckeen's shed.

Muckeen was as cold
as a packet of frozen peas,
but he gave a little squeal
of happiness.

He was going to be okay.
Mr Farmer had come
to save him.

He was not going to end up
like frozen food in a fridge.
Mrs Farmer arrived then.

Her nose and cheeks
were red and shiny
from the cold.
She didn't have Muckeen's
dinner with her.
She was carrying
a duvet and a torch
instead of a bucket.

'This is the worst
winter storm ever,'
said Mr Farmer.
'Oh it's terrible,'
said Mrs Farmer.
'I think there will be a
Big Freeze tonight.'

The weather was too cold
to leave Muckeen on his own
in the shed.

Mrs Farmer wrapped him
in the warm duvet.

She put a hat on his head.

'Muckeen is very cold,'
said Mrs Farmer.
'He will be grand when
we get him back to the house,'
said Mr Farmer.

Mrs Farmer carried Muckeen
all the way to the farmhouse
through the blizzard.

When they arrived
Muckeen was amazed.
The house was full!

There were:
sheep on the stairs

a horse in
the hall

cows in the kitchen

and chickens on the couch.

In front of a blazing fire
in the sitting room
sat the cat and the dog.

They were not pleased.

This was **their** house.
They did not want
to share it.
They wanted it
all to themselves.

But the other animals
were really happy.
They were glad that
Mr and Mrs Farmer
had brought them in
out of the cold.

For supper there was a selection of hay, oats and biscuits.

And at last
Muckeen got his
lovely bucket of
sloppy stuff.

When bedtime came,
the animals settled down
wherever they were.

But not Muckeen.

He was Mrs Farmer's
special pet.
Mrs Farmer
tucked him up
in the bed
in the spare room.

The bedclothes were
a bit too tight for Muckeen.

He missed his
lovely straw bed.

Still, the day had ended well.

Outside, the winter storm
blew all through the night.

Next morning,
everything looked different.
The storm was gone,
the sky was blue,
and the sun was shining.

Deep snow lay everywhere,
sparkling with frost.

As the animals woke up,
the house was
full of noise.
After breakfast,
they all went outside
to take a look at the snow.

First out
the door
were the ducks.

They hurried
down to the duck pond.
It was frozen.

Their flat feet were perfect
for skating on the ice.

Muckeen came skipping
down the stairs.
He was on his way out to play.
He saw Mr Farmer
searching in the cupboard
under the stairs.

Muckeen thought that
Mr Farmer might be looking
for field mice.

Mr Farmer was
muttering to himself:
'I know they're here
somewhere.'

Suddenly Mr Farmer
gave a happy shout.
'Here they are!'

He backed out of the cupboard.
He had two pairs of **skis**.
The skis had been
in the cupboard for years.

Muckeen could not
believe his eyes.
Real skis!

The farm was covered
in deep snow.
Skiing would be a good way
for Mr and Mrs Farmer
to get about.

Mr and Mrs Farmer
were great at skiing
when they were younger.

They even won
gold medals for it.

Muckeen jumped
up and down
with excitement.
He wanted to learn to ski.

So Mr Farmer
taught him how.

Soon he was off on his own,
speeding down the hill
in the Big Field.

His dream had come true.

Muckeen had a great time
in the snow.

He even made a snow pig.

Muckeen thought
the Big Freeze
was the best thing ever.